GET REAL!

The Trouble with...

by PHiL Kettle

ILLUStrated by
Melissa Webb

Get Real!
The Trouble with…

Written by Phil Kettle
Illustrations by Melissa Webb
Character design by David Dunstan

Text © 2009 Phil Kettle
Illustrations © 2009 Macmillan Education Australia Pty Ltd

Published by
Macmillan Education Australia Pty Ltd
Level 1, 15–19 Claremont Street, South Yarra,
Victoria 3141
www.macmillan.com.au

Edited by Emma Short

Designed by Jenny Lindstedt,
Goanna Graphics (Vic) Pty Ltd

Printed in China
10 9 8 7 6 5 4 3 2

ISBN: (pack) 9781420278828

ISBN: 9781420278255

Contents

Harry

Jesse

Introduction

The one on the right combing his hair is Jesse Harrison. The one on the left that isn't combing his hair is Harry Harvard.

The one in the middle looking really cross is Samantha Smithers. That's because she just washed her hair with dog flea wash. And if you want to know why, you have to keep reading this story.

The one standing behind Jesse, Harry and Sam is Harpo Whiney – the world-famous television interviewer. If you want to find out why Harpo Whiney is standing behind Jesse, Harry and Sam, then you have to keep reading this story. So get to it NOW!

Chapter One

The Harpo Show

"Hi there, and welcome to *The Harpo Show*. I'm Harpo Whiney and you're not – and with a name like Harpo, you might be very pleased that you're not!

Today you're in for a treat. We've got a show with a difference. I've left the comfort of my studio and have ventured here to this very ordinary town called Average. A lot of very bad things have been happening here."

"We're here today to interview Samantha Smithers. She is going to tell us why she has nominated Jesse Harrison and Harry Harvard in our worldwide contest to find the world's worst-behaved children.

I'm told that most of the bad things that have been happening in this very average town can somehow be traced back to these nominees, Jesse Harrison and Harry Harvard."

"Hello and welcome, Samantha Smithers!"

"Thank you, Harpo! It's so nice to meet you and to be on TV!"

"So, unfortunately you live in Normal Street. That's the same street as Jesse Harrison and Harry Harvard – which makes you neighbours."

"That's correct, Harpo."

"And are you also friends?"

"No way, Harpo!"

"What a shame!"

"Not really, Harpo! Straight up, I've got to say this. I don't like Jesse Harrison and I don't like Harry Harvard. I've nominated them as the world's worst-behaved children to expose them for what they really are…"

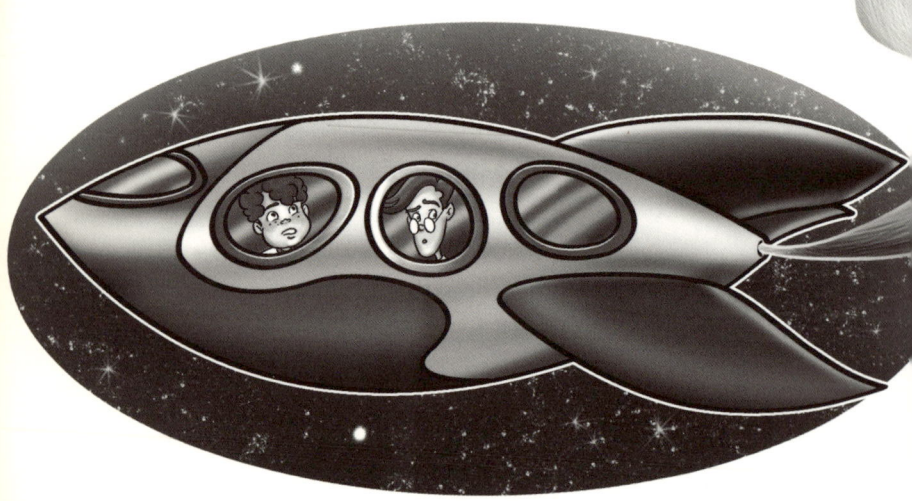

Chapter Two

Some Really Bad Stuff

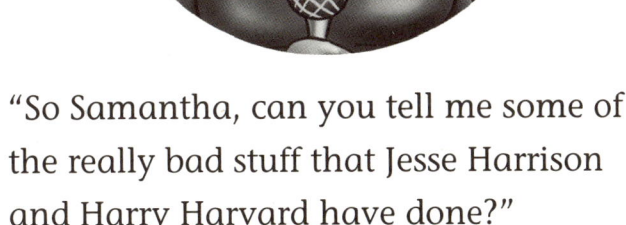

"So Samantha, can you tell me some of the really bad stuff that Jesse Harrison and Harry Harvard have done?"

Author Warning

I hope you're prepared to be **totally shocked** and I hope that you're sitting in a **comfortable** chair, because this interview could take a **really long time**. That's because Sam has so much to tell about the **really** bad stuff that Jesse and Harry have done.

I've lived in the same street as Jesse and Harry my entire life. If they're not IN trouble, then they're MAKING trouble. They have always been best friends. I don't think they have any other friends. They spend all their time together and sometimes I think they even know what each other is thinking. And none of what they're thinking is good.

The first really bad thing I remember was something they did to me when they first started school. One day, they'd been digging up worms from Jesse's garden. Apparently they were going to go fishing in the pond at the park but, for some strange reason, they changed their minds.

So instead of putting the worms back in the garden, like most normal people would, they put them in my lunchbox. When I opened my lunchbox I got such a big shock, I think I fainted on the spot.

And if that wasn't bad enough, then how about this? Another day, Jesse and Harry were speeding home from school through Average Park and they found a dead snake. They didn't just leave the snake where it was. They raced back to school and hid it in my locker.

eee

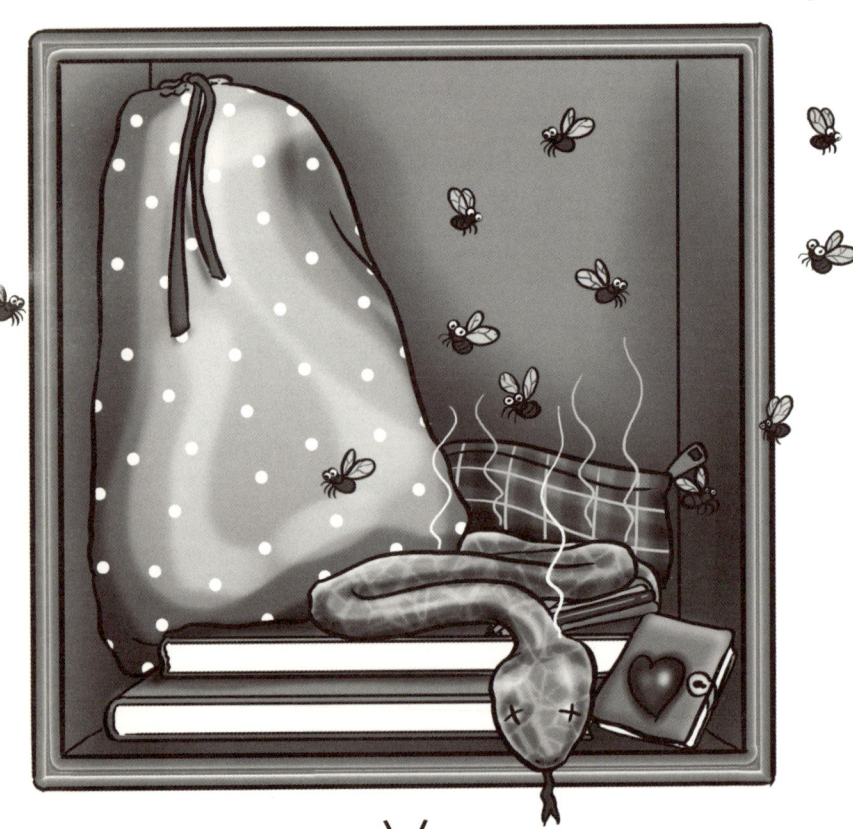

eeeeeeEEEEEEEEEEEEEEEEEEEEEEEEEEEEEEEEEEEEEEEEEEEEEK!

The next day, when I reached into my locker for my books, I pulled out this huge, ugly, DEAD snake. I screamed so loud and for so long that the entire population of Average heard me.

Chapter Three

More Really Bad Stuff

"My goodness, Samantha! This is amazing! Jesse Harrison and Harry Harvard are certainly worthy nominees for our contest. Can you tell me any more about what they have done?"

Last summer, Jesse and Harry took Jesse's father's golf clubs out of the garage to the park. I reckon Jesse and Harry think they're world champion golfers but the only thing they're world champions at is getting into trouble.

Somehow Jesse and Harry managed to hit all of Jesse's father's golf balls into the pond, and his golf clubs ended up in there too. I was watching and I saw everything they did.

Jesse and Harry got into so much trouble when I told Mr Harrison what they'd done! When Jesse and Harry asked me why I'd told Mr Harrison what they'd done, I told them that I did it for their own good.

I'm not sure that they believed me though. Maybe that was because I was laughing so hard when I told them.

The next day when I tried to ride to school on my bike, I found that both tyres were flat. I knew that Jesse and Harry had let the tyres down. When I asked them why, they told me that they did it for my own good. They said they didn't want me riding on the road and getting hit by a car.

I'm not sure that I believed them though. Maybe that was because they were laughing so hard when they told me.

Chapter four

The Tree House

"Well, that is just SO devious and dastardly! I don't know how you put up with these two boys. Can you tell us more?"

A NOTE FROM THE AUTHOR

Well, of course Sam can tell Harpo more!

Are you still sitting in that comfortable chair?

Maybe you should go and get something to eat.

If you're anything like Jesse and Harry, some

chips and peanut butter would be good!

Well, of course I can tell you more, Harpo! One day not that long ago, Jesse and Harry decided they were going to build a tree house in the big tree that separates Jesse's backyard from Harry's backyard. That was okay, except that they took all the palings from Mrs Brown's fence to build their tree house with.

I told them not to do it but they just wouldn't listen to me.

"She won't miss a few old palings!" they said.

"I think you might have taken a few too many!" I said.

Mrs Brown was away on holidays. When she got home, not only was her back fence gone, but so were all her chickens!

Mrs Brown was even crankier than usual.
Mr Harrison and Mr Harvard had to build her
a whole new fence. When it was finished, she
put a sign on it.

WARNING

KEEP
JESSE HARRISON
AND HARRY HARVARD
AWAY FROM MY
FENCE
OR ELSE!

When Jesse and Harry finished building their tree house, lots of strange things started happening. In fact, when Jesse and Harry are in their tree house, it's like they're in another world. I try not to spy on them when they're in their tree house, but sometimes I can't help wandering nearby and listening.

Lately I've heard Harry and Jesse talking about time a lot. They seem to think they've got a time machine, but I think they're just making it all up. Everybody knows that there's no such thing as a time machine. I think they need help. MAJOR HELP!

I've asked them to let me into their tree house, because I really want to see what happens in there. But they told me that it's their *tree house and no one else is allowed in*.

Chapter five

Crazy

"Jesse Harrison and Harry Harvard are truly badly behaved boys. They must drive you crazy, Samantha!"

Mrs Payne

Principal
Dorking

Jesse and Harry don't just drive me crazy,
Harpo. They drive everyone crazy – especially
Principal Dorking and Mrs Payne. She's their
Grade Five teacher at Average Primary School.

Jesse and Harry seem to think that school is boring. They act like it's their job to make sure that something interesting and funny is always happening. So they are ALWAYS getting in trouble and being sent to Principal Dorking's office. In fact, they've been in so much trouble, they practically live in Principal Dorking's office.

There was this one day when Jesse and Harry brought a cow to school. Not a little cow but a fully-grown cow, and a fully-grown cow is a really HUGE cow!

Jesse and Harry said they found the cow walking outside a paddock, but I think they found it inside the paddock. Then they put a rope around its neck and took it outside the paddock.

When Harry and Jesse eventually arrived at school, they were late as usual. And they were leading their fully-grown, really huge cow behind them. But instead of leaving the cow in the school yard, they took the cow right into Mrs Payne's classroom!

Jesse and Harry thought this was really funny, and that everybody would laugh. Actually, most of the class did laugh, except for Mrs Payne. She screamed so loud that she scared the cow out of its wits.

Then the cow did what most cows do when they get a fright. It lifted its tail and shot out the biggest cowpat you've ever seen. The cowpat went all over Mrs Payne's desk. Mrs Payne screamed again, even louder this time. And that was enough for the cow!

The cow decided that it wanted out. Eventually it found its way out of the classroom, down the corridor and towards the school gates. It was last seen running down the road outside the school.

Jesse and Harry were called into Principal Dorking's office, as usual. I just happened to be standing in the corridor outside and I heard every word that Principal Dorking said – or should I say every word that he screamed. I've never heard him so angry – and he's angry most of the time. Jesse and Harry got detention for two whole weeks!

Chapter Six

And Then...

...there was another day when Jesse and Harry snuck into Mr Zimmer's science laboratory and changed all the labels on the chemical containers. The next day, Mr Zimmer was showing our class how to make a volcano. He mixed all the chemicals he needed, or rather all the chemicals he THOUGHT he needed.

KABOOM!

The entire back wall of the science laboratory disappeared – and so did Mr Zimmer!

Principal Dorking was really mad. Jesse and Harry had to write two thousand lines.

We must learn to be good   We must learn to be good   We must
We must learn to be good   We must learn to be good   We mus
We must learn to be good   We must learn to be good   We mus
We must learn to be good   We must learn to be good   We mus
We must learn to be good   We must learn to be good   We must
We must learn to be good   We must learn to be good   We must
We must learn to be good   We must learn to be good   We mus
We must learn to be good   We must learn to be good   We must
We must learn to be good   We must learn to be good   We mus
We must learn to be good   We must learn to be good   We mus
We must learn to be good   We must learn to be good   We must
We must learn to be good   We must learn to be good   We mus
We must learn to be good   We must learn to be good   We must
We must learn to be good   We must learn to be good   We mus
We must learn to be good   We must learn to be good   We mus
We must learn to be good   We must learn to be good   We must
We must learn to be good   We must learn to be good   We mus
We must learn to be good   We must learn to be good   We mus
We must learn to be good   We must learn to be good   We mus
We must learn to be good   We must learn to be good   We mus
We must learn to be good   We must learn to be good   We mus
We must learn to be good   We must learn to be good   We mu
We must learn to be good   We must learn to be good   We mu
We must learn to be good   We must learn to be good   We mus
We must learn to be good   We must learn to be good   We mu
We must learn to be good   We must learn to be good   We mu

44

e good	we must learn to be good	We must learn to be good
De good	We must learn to be good	We must learn to be good
be good	we must learn to be good	We must learn to be good
De good	We must learn to be good	We must learn to be good
e good	we must learn to be good	We must learn to be good
e good	we must learn to be good	We must learn to be good
De good	we must learn to be good	We must learn to be good
e good	we must learn to be good	We must learn to be good
be good	we must learn to be good	We must learn to be good
De good	we must learn to be good	We must learn to be good
e good	we must learn to be good	We must learn to be good
De good	we must learn to be good	We must learn to be good
e good	we must learn to be good	We must learn to be good
be good	we must learn to be good	We must learn to be good
De good	we must learn to be good	We must learn to be good
e good	we must learn to be good	We must learn to be good
De good	we must learn to be good	We must learn to be good
be good	we must learn to be good	We must learn to be good
be good	we must learn to be good	We must learn to be good
De good	we must learn to be good	We must learn to be good
be good	we must learn to be good	We must learn to be good
be good	we must learn to be good	We must learn to be good
be good	we must learn to be good	We must learn to be good
be good	we must learn to be good	We must learn to be good
be good	we must learn to be good	We must learn to be good
be good	we must learn to be good	We must learn to be good
.be good	we must learn to be good	We must learn to be good

Chapter Seven

The Great Nit Invasion

"So tell us, Samantha. Did Harry and Jesse finally learn to be good?"

Of course not, Harpo. The worst thing that ever happened in our school was the great nit invasion, and Jesse and Harry were right in the thick of it. Okay, maybe they weren't totally responsible, but they certainly helped turn it into total chaos.

A REMINDER FROM THE AUTHOR

Actually, there was also the attack of the giant ferret — but that's another story called **Ferret Attack**! And then there was the trip to Big City Museum — but that's another story called **Big City Museum**! And then there was the incident with the flying machines — but that's another story called **The Flying Machines**! And then there was...oh forget it, we could be here all day!

One day last term, I was helping out in Mrs Payne's Grade Five classroom. All the Grade Five kids were trying to stay awake, when suddenly Lenny 'the Stink' Edwards started to scratch his head. He just couldn't seem to stop scratching.

Jesse, who was watching Lenny as he scratched, yelled out at the top of his voice,

"NIT ATTACK! NIT ATTACK!"

Mrs Payne grabbed a comb and ran it through Lenny 'the Stink' Edwards' hair.

"Yep, you've got nits!" she said, and then she smiled. "Line up children – it's time for a NIT CHECK!"

As the kids lined up, the nits started to leap from Lenny 'the Stink' Edwards' head to all the other kids' heads. Then all the kids started to scratch. There was leaping and scratching and leaping and scratching until the whole classroom turned into a scratching leaping nit circus!

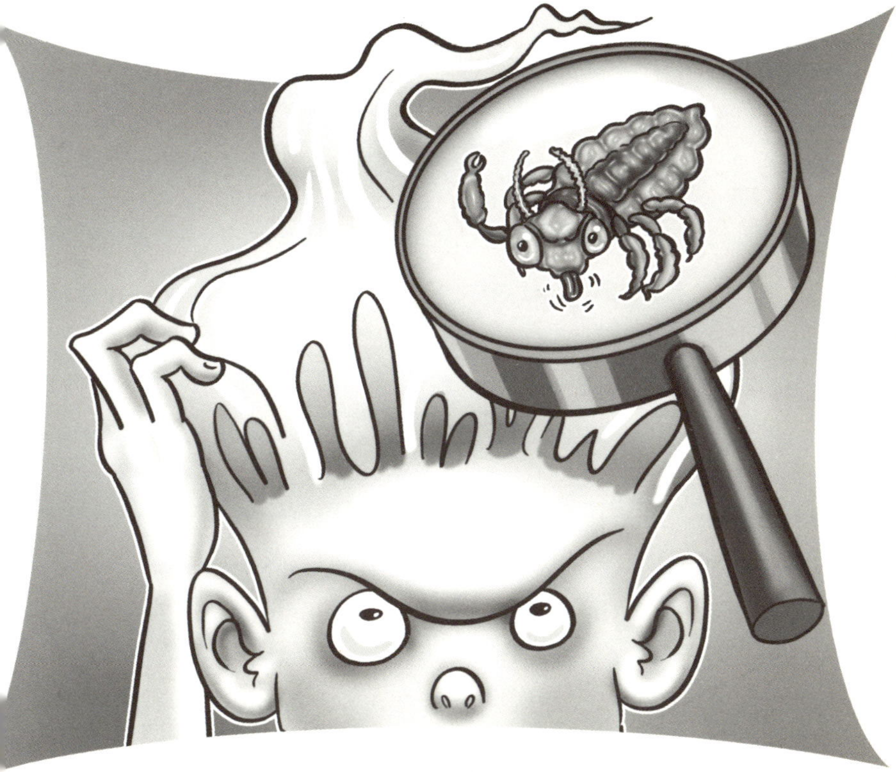

Chapter eight

More Nits!

That's when Jesse and Harry got the idea for what they did next. They sat down at the computer and wrote a newsletter.

BEWARE!

NITS HAVE INVADED AVERAGE PRIMARY SCHOOL. ALL STUDENTS AND THEIR PARENTS ARE REQUIRED TO WASH THEIR HAIR WITH DOG FLEA WASH AND REPORT TO PRINCIPAL DORKING TOMORROW MORNING.

P.S. DOG FLEA WASH IS AVAILABLE IN ALL GOOD PET SHOPS AND EVEN IN BAD PET SHOPS.

Signed: ....

Jesse and Harry, who are really good at being sneaky, went to Principal Dorking's office and knocked on his door. When Principal Dorking asked why they had been sent there this time, Jesse and Harry told him that they weren't *in trouble.*

They said that they were only there because sometime in the next twelve months, it was going to be Mrs Payne's birthday. They said they had made Mrs Payne a birthday card and were sure that he'd want to sign it.

Principal Dorking picked up a pen and signed without reading what was on the card – but it *wasn't a card,* it was the newsletter. Then Jesse and Harry snuck into the photocopying room and made enough copies of the newsletter for every student in the school.

53

Not even Jesse and Harry could believe the TOTAL CHAOS that the newsletter caused. The whole town of Average went into total meltdown. Everybody was affected. The pet shops sold out of dog flea wash. And the sound of screaming children echoed all over Average, because none of them wanted their hair washed with dog flea wash.

Principal Dorking was interviewed by Scoop Jones from the Average Daily News. *He said that he didn't know anything about the nit invasion OR the newsletter that had been sent to all the students from Average Primary School. Nobody believed him because his signature was on the newsletter.*

Everybody in Average was scratching and itching and scratching some more. Jesse and Harry were the only two people in Average who were totally unaware of all the itching and scratching that was going on.

When Harry and Jesse arrived at school the next morning, late as usual, they were in HUGE trouble. But at least they'd *had a good night's sleep.*

Principal Dorking was hiding under his desk. He was itching and scratching and trying to avoid all the angry parents that had stormed the school. The angry parents were itching and scratching too.

Soon he felt brave enough to come out from under his desk – plus it was pretty hard itching and scratching in such a small space. He saw Jesse and Harry arrive from his office window. They were the only ones NOT itching and scratching.

Principal Dorking stuck his head out his office door. In a BOOMING and really scary *voice, he told Jesse and Harry to report to his office IMMEDIATELY. Jesse and Harry got into the BIGGEST trouble ever. Actually, they got into so much trouble that they were suspended for two whole weeks.*

But that was so unfair – not because
they were suspended, but because they got
to spend two whole weeks playing in the
park and hanging out in their tree house.
Meanwhile the rest of us had to go to school!

Chapter Nine

That's All Folks!

"Gee Samantha, thank you for telling us all about Jesse Harrison and Harry Harvard. I'm sure that my audience now understands why you've nominated them in our international contest to find the worst-behaved boys in the world! This is Harpo Whiney, signing off from Average."

"But look! Here comes Jesse and Harry now. Jesse and Harry, Samantha Smithers has nominated you in our international contest to find the worst-behaved boys in the world. What have you got to say about that?"

"GET REAL!"

Let's Write

Getting to Know Your Characters

Now you're really into planning your story! You've got a list of ideas and you've used visualisation to build up a word picture of your location. The next thing you need to think about is the characters that you would like to have in your story.

I spend more time planning my characters than on anything else. You need to know your characters well. In fact, creating new characters is a lot like making new friends. You get to know what they look like, how they think, what they like, what they don't like…all the things that make them unique and special. So open up your creative-writing book and on the top of a new page, write:

My story plan - ideas

Think of a character that you might like to have in your story and write down everything you need to know about that character.

Name: Favourite food:

Age: Favourite sports:

Hair colour: Friends:

Family members: Pets:

Likes: Hobbies:

Dislikes:

Start planning your characters now. And remember, you need to know every single thing that 'makes them tick'!

Jesse and Harry Present

About the Author

Jesse: So Phil, how do you think the other students would have described you when you were at school?

Phil: *They would have said that I was a really nice person who did everything he was told.*

Jesse: Are you sure?

Phil: *Well, maybe there was the odd time that I didn't do exactly what I was told.*

Jesse: Like what?

Phil: *Once I took a pigeon to school in my school bag. The teacher wasn't very impressed. And there was another time I found a dead snake on my way home from school. I put it in my sister's bed. I got into major trouble for that.*

Jesse: So Phil, it seems to me like you might have got into a lot of trouble when you were at school.

Phil: *No way! I was a perfect child.*

About the Illustrator

Harry: *Hey Melissa, did you ever get into trouble when you were at school?*

Melissa: *Well Harry, I do remember being told by the principal, that if I didn't "pull my socks up" I might like to go to school somewhere else. Who knows why?*

Harry: *How did you learn to draw nits? They're so tiny!*

Melissa: *I have been blessed by experience and a pair of glasses.*

Word-up!

Shin: what you use to find furniture in the dark

Stick: a boomerang that doesn't come back

Teenager: someone whose hang-ups do not include clothes

Tornado: an ending with a twist

Truth: something that doesn't lie in the open

Yawn: an honest opinion openly expressed

Disrupt: what Jesse and Harry do better than most

A Laugh a Minute!

Why was the broom late for school?
It over-swept!

What did the firefighter's wife get for Christmas?
A ladder in her stocking!

What runs but never walks?
Water!

How do you make a milk shake?
Give it a good scare!

Why did the clock get sick?
It was run down!

Which cheese is made backwards?
Edam!

Other Titles in the Series